OWL'S Tale

Elaine L. Anderson

This book is dedicated to my parents, Jean and Stanley
Robertson, for all their unfailing love.

*Elaine Anderson is an infant teacher
and a practising Baptist. Her husband is a lecturer
and they have two children.*

Illustrated by Lee Gallaher

Copyright © Elaine L. Anderson 1991

First published 1991

Printed and published by The Stanborough Press Limited
for Autumn House Publications, Alma Park, Grantham, NG31 9SL, England.

ISBN 0-904748-69-3

Everybody knows that owls are wise. The owl who lived in Wrangle Wood was no different. He was so wise that he knew all about Jesus. He could quote huge chunks of the Bible. Sometimes, at parties, he would recite the twenty-third Psalm very quickly. He was often asked to do that because everybody loved it.

One windy night as Owl sat next to his fire, saying his prayers, he heard a faint tap at the door. At first he thought it was only the wind, but then he heard it again, only this time it was louder. He went to the door and looked through the peep-hole to see who it was. There was Squirrel, shivering on the doorstep, pulling his large fluffy tail round him.

'Oh, what does he want?' thought Owl as he opened the door to Squirrel.

'Come in! Come in, quickly now!' said Owl.

Squirrel scuttled inside. Owl put on his spectacles and peered at Squirrel.

'What can I do for you, Squirrel?' he asked.

Squirrel rubbed his nose with his paw, and began:

'Well, I seem to have lost my supply of nuts. I was sure I buried them at the bottom of the big oak tree, but I can't find them, and I've tried at the side of the gate near that old oil drum, but they're not there either. I just don't know what I've done with them.'

'Tut!' said Owl, glaring down his beak at Squirrel. 'I seem to remember the same thing happening last year.'

'Come and sit down', said Owl, pointing his wing to the large table in the middle of the room. Squirrel sat down.

'Now, let's see', said Owl. 'If my memory serves me right, last year we drew a map, and then you tried to remember where you went. We'll draw another map!'

Owl pulled open the drawer at the end of the table and brought out a large sheet of white paper.

'Now, where did you gather the nuts?'

Squirrel wasn't listening. He was looking at the large bowl of acorns on the table. He could smell their lovely woody, nutty smell, and his mouth started to water. His tummy was rumbling too, for he had eaten nothing for two days.

'Squirrel!'

Owl's voice made him jump.

'Eh? Yes?' said Squirrel, turning to Owl, who looked rather cross.

'Squirrel, are you listening? I said, "Where did you gather the nuts?"'

'Oh, well, I gathered some in the big trees by the farm, and I think I gathered some near Coppins Glade.'

'Mmmm. Yes', said Owl, as he started to write on the paper. He grunted, and muttered a few things under his breath, and did a lot of measuring with a large ruler.

At last he slapped his wing on the table and shouted:

'Eureka! I've found it! You must have buried them in the Glade just after you picked them!'

Squirrel looked at the map. Owl had made a large red cross where he was sure the nuts would be found.

'I'm sure that if you go back and search the Glade the nuts will be there, Squirrel.'

Owl smiled kindly at Squirrel as he handed him the map.

'But even if you don't, Squirrel, remember the words of our good Lord, "Life is more important than food".'

Squirrel nodded. He was too tired and weak with hunger to reply. Owl led him to the door.

'I do hope you find the nuts, Squirrel', said Owl in a kind voice.

'Thank you for your help, Owl', said Squirrel quietly. 'Good night.'

'Don't mention it, Squirrel. I love helping people! God bless!'

Owl's Tree

Squirrel's
Tree

The
Glade

Owl went back to his fire and, drawing his chair up close, he picked up his Bible and began to pray:

'Thank you, Jesus, for making me wise and not stupid and forgetful like Squirrel. And thank you, Lord, that I can be of so much help to the others.'

Owl picked up a few acorns from the table, and started to nibble them while he read his Bible. No sooner had he started, however, than he heard another tap at his door.

'Goodness me! Goodness me!' he said, looking at the clock. 'Whoever is it now?'

He went to the door and looked through the peep-hole, and there stood Mrs. Robin on the doorstep with her three little ones tucked under her wings.

'Oh dear! Oh dear!' thought Owl. 'More problems for me to solve I shouldn't wonder.'

Mrs. Robin and her little ones hopped inside, and Owl shut the door quickly.

'Whatever is the matter, Mrs. Robin?' said Owl. 'Isn't it late to have the children out visiting?'

'Oh!' wailed Mrs. Robin, and she began to tell her tale.

'It's my nest. Blown down, hasn't it! The wind! Oh!'

Mrs. Robin started wailing again. The little ones were wet through and started shaking themselves, sending showers of dirty water all over the room.

'Steady on!' said Owl in a stern voice, looking at them with a very owly stare. 'Go and sit on the spare bed over there, while I talk to your mother.'

The chicks hopped over to the far corner of the room and, one by one, jumped up onto the bed, where they huddled up to each other to keep warm. Owl turned to Mrs. Robin:

'Now, calm down, and let's talk about this. Your home has blown down, right?'

'Yes', sniffed Mrs. Robin into her hankie.

'And you've nowhere to sleep tonight?'

'No, (sniff) and my poor babies will be cold and wet outside without a nest. They might catch a chill and die (sniff). Ooh, it's terrible, terrible!' Mrs. Robin gave another long wail.

'Now, please do calm down, Mrs. Robin. This is not helping at all! Luckily you've come to the right place for help. Your babies will be fine.'

Mrs. Robin looked across to where the chicks were lying cuddled up and asleep once more, like three balls of cotton wool.

'Oh (sniff) thank you, Owl', she said.

'Yes. I know just the place for you', said Owl. 'There's an old nest in the hawthorn hedge down the road. I saw it only yesterday. It's a bit tatty, and needs some repairs, but it's somewhere for you and the children to spend the night. Come back in the morning and I'll lend you a book on nest building. It's the best to be found. I should know, I wrote it!'

'That's very kind of you', said Mrs. Robin in a tired voice.

She gathered up her sleepy chicks once more and stood in Owl's doorway watching the driving rain and biting wind.

'Now do stop worrying, Mrs. Robin. Have faith in our Heavenly Father! He will provide for you,' said Owl.

'Thank you, Owl', she said as she tucked her little ones under her wings, and put her head down to battle against the wind.

'No trouble at all!' shouted Owl, trying to make himself heard above the noise of the gale. 'I love helping people!'

Owl smiled and closed the door. He shivered.

'Brrrr. It really is quite chilly out there tonight', he thought as he popped another log on the fire. He settled himself down again in his chair. Then, holding his Bible in his lap, he closed his eyes and began to pray:

'Thank you, Lord, for making me so calm and sensible, not nervous like Mrs. Robin. And thank you, Lord, for my wonderful eyesight that helps me to spot things like that nest for Mrs. Robin.'

Owl smiled. It really gave him great joy to share his wisdom with others. He looked across to the corner of the room where the spare bed was now looking very untidy.

'Really!' thought Owl. 'What a mess to leave it in!'

He was so tired he thought about leaving it till the morning to tidy it up, but then changed his mind.

'Better do it now, in case our Heavenly Father should send someone else to shelter from the storm.'

As he was tidying the bed he heard a funny sort of snuffling noise coming from the door. He walked over and looked through the peep-hole but there was nothing to see. He went back to making the bed. Again he heard the noise. He went over to the door. This time he opened it. As he did so in rolled Hedgehog with a bump. He had been leaning on the door, crying.

'What are you doing, hanging around my door at this time of night?' asked Owl, closing the door.

'I'm so sad', said Hedgehog in a weak little voice. 'I don't have any friends. I can't seem to get close to people. I've got no one to talk to. I'm sure nobody loves me. I saw your 'God is love' sticker in the window and thought you might help me.'

'Well I'd better pray for you, I suppose', said Owl, sighing. 'OK?'

'OK', said Hedgehog.

'The question is, which prayer? We must pray the right prayer or it might not work. I've got this really good prayer that might work.'

Owl looked at Hedgehog. He was in a sorry state. His feet were dirty and caked with mud. Some leaves and a bright orange chewing-gum paper were stuck to his prickles, and since he had come in Owl had noticed a rather nasty smell.

'Yes', thought Owl, Hedgehog does look in a bad way.

'Hang on. Before we pray, could you just stand on this?' said Owl, laying a large sheet of brown paper on the rug in front of Hedgehog.

'Does standing on brown paper help God to hear our prayers?' asked Hedgehog.

'Don't be silly, Hedgehog, of course not', said Owl. 'It's to save my carpet from getting muddy — your feet are really filthy!'

Hedgehog scuttled onto the brown paper.

'Now before we start, Hedgehog,' said Owl in a firm voice, 'there's one thing we must get straight. You must get rid of this silly idea that you are not loved. Our Heavenly Father loves us all — short and tall, big and small, little and spiky!' He stamped on a large flea which had just leaped from Hedgehog's back.

Owl put on his glasses again, and read from a large book called, *Prayers for the Poor in Spirit*.

'Right, Hedgehog, are you lonely, unhappy, far-from-home, or needing help in any way?' he asked.

Hedgehog nodded.

'Well, which?' asked Owl.

'All of them', said Hedgehog.

'Well you can't have all these prayers tonight',

answered Owl. 'Have you seen how long they are? We'll be here all night! You'll have to choose one.'

'Oh, I can't', said Hedgehog. 'You pick.'

'OK', said Owl, looking for the shortest one. 'This seems a nice prayer, the "Far-from-home" one.'

'Fine', said Hedgehog. 'What do I do?'

'Nothing', said Owl. 'I'll do it. Just close your eyes and think about God.'

Hedgehog closed his eyes tight.

'Ready?' asked Owl.

'No!' said Hedgehog.

'What's the matter now?' asked Owl, getting a bit ruffled.

'Well, I can't think about God because I don't know what He looks like. I've never seen Him.'

'Oh', sighed Owl. 'Hedgehog, don't you know *anything*?'

'Not a lot', said Hedgehog as a large tear plopped onto the brown paper. 'I told you I was stupid. Nobody loves me because I'm stupid.'

'Oh, don't start all that again', said Owl. 'Look!' Owl took his Bible off the chair and found a colour picture of Jesus feeding people by the sea.

'That's Jesus. The one with the beard and the long white robe', he said, showing the picture to Hedgehog.

'Oh, Him!' said Hedgehog. 'I've seen Him! He's outside!'

'Don't be silly!' said Owl, who was beginning to wonder if it was worth praying for Hedgehog at all.

'This picture is very old. He's not around any more. And he's certainly *not* outside.'

'I'm sure it's Him', said Hedgehog. 'I saw Him before I came here. He's knocking on people's doors and telling them He loves them.'

'Hedgehog!' shouted Owl. 'I will remind you that this is our Gracious Heavenly Saviour we are talking about, not some door-to-door salesman. Either show respect or leave my home.' He shook his wing angrily, pointing to the door.

'Sorry,' said Hedgehog, 'but Owl, if it's not Jesus it's somebody very much like Him, and He's got Squirrel and Mrs. Robin with Him.'

'Oh, no!' said Owl. 'Have I not told them a thousand times not to go with strangers? Well, it's their own fault if they don't listen to me. Now close your eyes, Hedgehog, and I'll pray for you. I think I'll just pray a little home-made prayer tonight. I'll pray a proper one tomorrow when I'm not so tired.'

Hedgehog closed his eyes.

Owl started to pray:

'Dearest Lord, help our poor brother Hedgehog. Let him know that you love him as much as you love me.' (Owl didn't think this possible, but he thought he would say it all the same as it might cheer Hedgehog up.) 'And while you're at it, Lord,' said Owl, looking sideways at Hedgehog, 'could you maybe change Hedgehog into something a bit more lovable?'

Owl wondered if he should have added that last bit. Changing Hedgehog into something lovable was an awful lot to ask, even of God.

'Amen', said Owl.

'Amen', said Hedgehog.

'There now, feel any better?' asked Owl.

'No, not really', said Hedgehog.

'Well, prayer does sometimes take a long time', said Owl. 'I expect when God hears He'll send you down a whole lot of happiness, and perhaps someone to talk to.'

Owl opened the door. 'Good night, Hedgehog.'

Hedgehog didn't want to go.

'Couldn't I stay a little longer and talk to you, Owl?' he asked.

'Talk to me! Talk to me!' Owl shouted, getting rather cross. 'What do you think we've been doing for the last half hour?'

'Sorry', said Hedgehog.

'A lot of people expect me to help them, you know', said Owl. 'I can't do that if I don't get my sleep, can I?'

'No', said Hedgehog, as he wearily made his way out of the door.

Owl decided to go to bed to do his Bible reading. As he was getting in he noticed that the orange sticky chewing-gum wrapper was no longer on Hedgehog's spine. It was now stuck to the sole of his own foot.

'Oh, Yuk!' said Owl as he lay back on his bed. It wasn't always easy being kind and helpful, he thought to himself as he got out his Bible and began to read:

'You must always be ready, for the Son of Man will come at an hour when you do not expect Him.'

'Good idea,' thought Owl. 'Always to be ready.' In fact he thought it was such a good idea that he got his pen and drew a line under the words. Then he wrote 'Very wise' beside it.

Owl thought it sad that only *he* knew about Jesus and about getting ready.

'What a shame,' he thought, 'that the other creatures don't know about Jesus. They won't be ready.'

Just then there was a loud knock on the door.

'Go away!' shouted Owl, 'I'm busy', as he went on reading his Bible.

The knock came again.

'It's very late!' shouted Owl. 'I'm too tired for visitors. Come back tomorrow.'

When the knocking came a third time, Owl really lost his temper and flew out of bed to the door. As he looked through the peep-hole he saw the stranger that Hedgehog had told him about.

'Look here, I don't know who you are, or what you're selling,' he shouted through the peep-hole, 'but I don't want any!'

'Owl, it's me, Jesus', said the stranger.

Owl looked again through the peep-hole.

The man certainly looked like Jesus. In fact the more Owl looked, the more he thought that it *was* Jesus. Owl flung open the door.

'Come in! Come in!' said Owl, all excited. 'You needn't have knocked! I've just been *reading* about you!'

'Didn't you know it was me, Owl?' Jesus asked.

'Er, well, it's a very small peep-hole', said Owl. 'Come on in and sit down.'

Jesus stepped in.

'You've come to the right place', said Owl with a grin. 'I know all about you. I know all about being ready!'

'That's what you may think, Owl,' said Jesus, 'but you don't *really* know me at all.'

'Er, pardon?' said Owl, and his eyes opened wide.

'You know all *about me*, Owl, but you don't know *me*', said Jesus. 'If you really knew me you would have fed my squirrel, not shown him where to find nuts, and you would have sheltered my robin and her babies, not sent them out in the cold to look for a nest. You should have *loved* my hedgehog for me, while you prayed. Didn't you know that "Love one another" is the greatest of all my commandments?'

'I forgot', said Owl, looking down. He felt awful. Here he was all this time thinking he was so wise, and he didn't know Jesus' greatest commandment.

'Please forgive me, Jesus', Owl said quietly.

'I forgive you', said Jesus.

Owl thought about his friends, Squirrel, Mrs. Robin, and Hedgehog. How badly he had treated them! If only he could call them back and ask them to forgive him too.

Just then he heard a familiar snuffling noise and, as he looked up, Hedgehog scuttled from behind Jesus and stood in front of Owl looking up at him, his little eyes shining and twinkling. Squirrel tiptoed from under Jesus' cloak and stood next to Hedgehog. Then Jesus gently lifted Mrs. Robin and her babies from inside His sleeve and put them down at Owl's feet.

Owl smiled and spread his wings over them.

'Please, please, forgive me, dear friends', he said. 'I have been stupid. Can we start all over again?'

They all nodded and smiled at him.

'We forgive you, Owl', they said.

Jesus stood up and smiled.

'I've got to go now, but always remember what I've told you tonight. "Love one another".'

'Don't worry, Jesus. I won't forget!' said Owl.

And he never did.